The Grosset Treasury of
Nursery Tales

The Grosset Treasury of
Nursery Tales

Pictures by Tadasu Izawa and Shigemi Hijikata

Publishers · GROSSET & DUNLAP · New York

Contents

Library of Congress Catalog Card Number: 77-71717
ISBN : 0-448-12289-8

Illustrations Copyright © 1967, 1968, 1969, 1971, 1977 by Tadasu Izawa and Shigemi Hijikata
through management of Dairisha, Inc. Printed and bound in Japan
by Zokeisha Publications, Ltd., Roppongi, Minato-ku, Tokyo.

Henny-Penny

One day Henny-Penny was picking up corn in the barnyard when — WHACK! — something hit her upon the head.

"Goodness gracious me!" said Henny-Penny. "The sky is going to fall! I must go and tell the king."

So she went along and went along till she met Cocky-Locky, who asked her where she was going.

"I'm going to tell the king the sky is falling."

"May I come with you?" said Cocky-Locky.

"Certainly," said Henny-Penny.

So they went along and went along till they met Ducky-Daddles, who asked them where they were going.

"We're going to tell the king the sky is falling."

"May I come with you?" said Ducky-Daddles.

"Certainly," said Henny-Penny and Cocky-Locky.

So they went along and went along till they met Goosey-Poosey, who asked where they were going.

"We're going to tell the king the sky is falling."

"May I come with you?" said Goosey-Poosey.

"Certainly," said Henny-Penny, Cocky-Locky and Ducky-Daddles.

So they went along and went along till they met Turkey-Lurkey, who asked them where they were going.

"We're going to tell the king the sky is falling."
"May I come with you?" said Turkey-Lurkey.

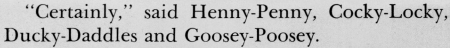

"Certainly," said Henny-Penny, Cocky-Locky, Ducky-Daddles and Goosey-Poosey.

So they went along and went along till they met Foxy-Woxy, who asked them where they were going.

"We're going to tell the king the sky is falling," said Henny-Penny, Cocky-Locky, Ducky-Daddles, Goosey-Poosey and Turkey-Lurkey.

13

Just behind him was the door of Foxy-Woxy's hillside cave. Foxy-Woxy said to Henny-Penny, Cocky-Locky, Ducky-Daddles, Goosey-Poosey and Turkey-Lurkey, "This is the short way to the king's palace. You will soon get there if you follow me. I will go first, and you come after."

"Why, of course, certainly, without doubt, why not?" said Henny-Penny, Cocky-Locky, Ducky-Daddles, Goosey-Poosey and Turkey-Lurkey.

So Foxy-Woxy went into his cave. He didn't go far, but turned around to wait for Henny-Penny, Cocky-Locky, Ducky-Daddles, Goosey-Poosey and Turkey-Lurkey.

Turkey-Lurkey was the first to go into the dark hole of the cave. Then followed Goosey-Poosey, Ducky-Daddles and Cocky-Locky. And each one was pounced upon and gobbled up by Foxy-Woxy.

But Cocky-Locky will always crow, and he had time for one big "Cock-a-doodle-doo!" before Henny-Penny could enter the cave.

When Henny-Penny heard Cocky-Locky crow, she said to herself, "My goodness! It must be dawn. Time for me to lay my egg!"

So Henny-Penny turned right around and bustled off. And she never DID tell the king the sky was falling.

The Three Little Pigs

There were once three little pigs who lived with their mother.

One of them was fond of music, and he spent his time playing a guitar and singing. The second pig liked nothing better than to dance the whole day long. But the third little pig was happiest helping his mother in any way he could.

One day the mother pig decided her children were old enough to take care of themselves. So she gave each of them a gold piece and sent them out into the world.

"Don't worry, Mother," said the third little pig. "I'll look after my brothers." And off they trotted to seek their fortunes.

"First we must have houses to live in," said the wise little pig, and he promptly bought a load of bricks to build his house.

"Ho, ho," laughed his brothers. "Bricks are much too heavy." So the first foolish pig bought a load of straw to build his house. The second foolish pig bought some sticks and some boards.

"How silly you are!" said the wise little pig. "When the wolf comes after you, he will blow your houses away with one puff." But his brothers paid no attention to him.

The wise little pig was soon busy building his house of bricks.

"Oh, let's play awhile before we go to work," said his brothers. And they spent the whole day singing and dancing while the wise pig worked away.

"You had better hurry," he warned his brothers. "Night is

coming, and you'll be singing a different tune when the wolf comes looking for you."

At last the first little pig put down his guitar, and in a very short time he had built a house of straw for himself. "Now I don't have a thing to worry about," he said proudly. And he popped inside and shut the door.

Soon along came the wolf. He knocked loudly on the first little pig's door, saying, "Little pig, little pig, let me come in!" Trying to sound brave, the little pig replied, "Not by the hair of my chinny-chin-chin!"

"Then I'll huff and I'll puff and I'll BLOW your house in!" said the wolf. So he huffed and he puffed and he blew the first little pig's house right down!

Off ran the frightened pig as fast as he could to his brother, whose house was built of sticks and boards. He had just finished nailing it together when the first little pig arrived on his doorstep, all out of breath and crying, "Help, help, the wolf is **after** me!" Quickly the two little pigs popped inside the house and shut the door tight.

The wolf soon arrived and knocked loudly on the door, saying in a fierce voice, "Little pig, little pig, let me come in!" And in a trembling voice the second pig replied, "Not by the hair of my chinny-chin-chin!"

"Then I'll huff and I'll puff and I'll BLOW your house in!"

So he huffed and he puffed, and he blew down the house of sticks and boards, and sent the two little pigs flying. They picked themselves up and raced off as fast as their legs would carry them to their brother's house.

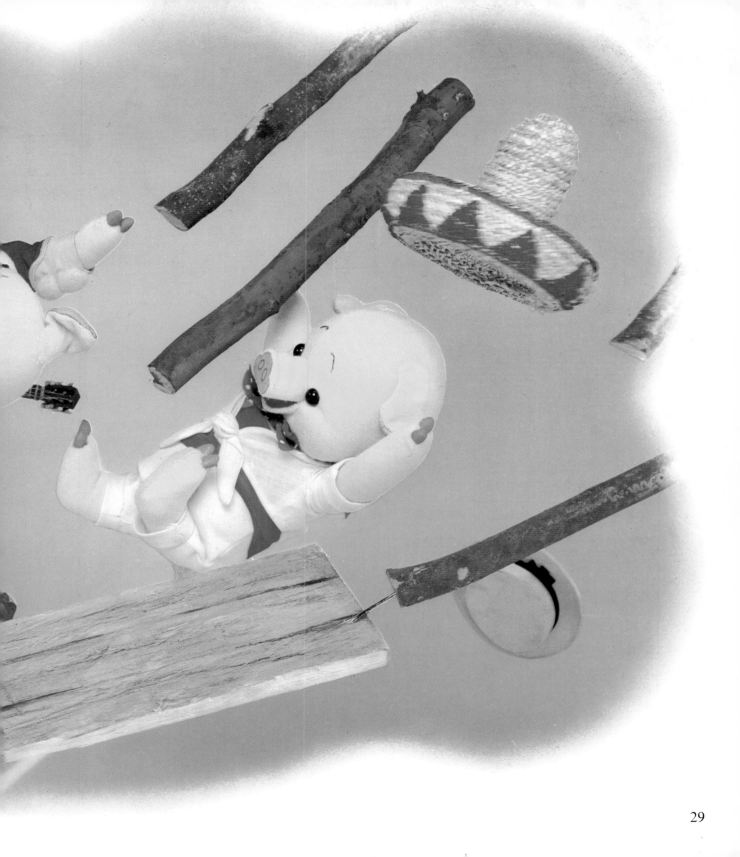

The wise little pig had finished building his house of bricks and was sitting outside, enjoying the cool evening breeze. Suddenly he saw his two brothers running toward him, with the wolf close behind. Quick as a wink the three little pigs popped into the house of bricks and slammed the door.

The wolf was very angry, indeed! He pounded on the door, howling, "Little pig, little pig, let me come in!"

The wise little pig replied, "Not by the hair of my chinny-chin-chin!"

"Then I'll huff and I'll puff and I'll BLOW your house in!" shouted the wolf. So he huffed and he puffed, and he puffed and he huffed, but he couldn't blow down the house of bricks.

"I'll get those three fat little pigs," muttered the wolf to himself. "I'll drop down the chimney and catch them by surprise."

But the wise little pig saw the wolf climbing up the drainpipe toward the roof. He quickly lit a hot fire in the fireplace and put on a large kettle to boil.

Rumble-tumble-splash! Down fell the wolf into the boiling water in the kettle.

"Now, foolish brothers," said the wise little pig, "you have learned your lesson. Let's all live together here in my house of bricks." So while the first little pig played his guitar and the second little pig danced, the wise little pig cooked a delicious supper for them all.

The Ugly Duckling

Bits of eggshell lay scattered about as the last of a brood of baby ducklings stepped out of his shell and blinked at the world one sunny spring morning. "At last!" exclaimed his mother. "But such a scrawny one you are! Well, come along now. We are all going for a swim."

After they had all splashed in the pond for a while, the mother duck led her downy brood back to the barnyard to show them off.

The youngest lagged behind. His feet were clumsy, his neck was much too long, and he had such a big bill! All agreed that her ducklings were finer than ever this year. "But what a pity," said one old rooster, "that that one should be so ugly!"

The poor duckling tried to hide, but wherever he went, the chickens pecked at him, the turkeys chased him, and even the milkmaid shooed him out of her way.

Finally, one day he could stand it no more, and, seeing the barnyard gate ajar, the ugly duckling set forth on his journey.

Not far away he met two young wild geese in a marsh. Perhaps he could go along with them.

But before the duckling could open his mouth, the geese flew upward with a great whirring of wings. A shot rang out and one

bird fell dead in the water. The startled duckling scooted into the reeds near the shore where, all through the long afternoon, while the hunters aimed at the wild birds, he cowered in his hiding-place. But he had nothing to fear, for even when one of the hunt-er's dogs found him among the cattails, he sniffed just once and left him alone because he was so ugly.

When darkness came, the duckling slipped out of the marsh and made his way to a humble cottage, where he found an old woman living alone with her hen and her cat. But since he could neither lay eggs nor arch his back and purr in her lap, they had little use for him.

Soon the duckling had had quite enough, and so set forth once more.

41

For a while he spent his days swimming and diving by the shores of a lake. But the falling leaves and chill winds of autumn warned that winter would soon come.

One brisk morning the duckling looked up to see three large white swans fly past on their way to warmer lands. He longed to join them. But, alas, wasn't he too small and ugly?

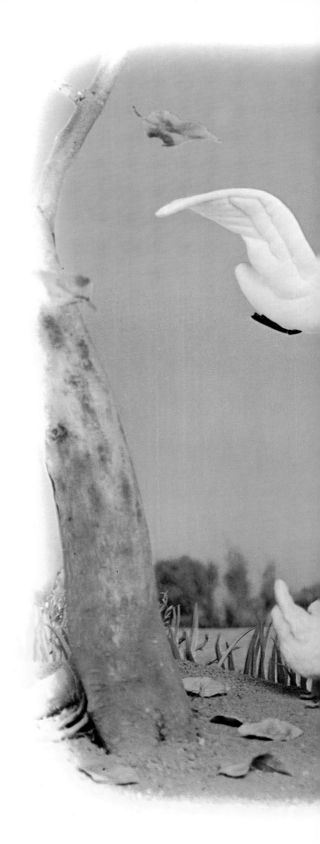

Now each day was colder than the last. A lacy blanket of snow-flakes covered the ground and slowly the ice spread over the lake. The poor duckling swam in circles from morning to night, trying to keep one small place open. But one morning he awoke to find himself frozen fast. Fortunately, a woodsman came along and, seeing the poor bird's plight, chopped him out of the ice with his ax and carried him home under his arm.

But the duckling had no sooner dried his feathers by the fire than the woodsman's little girl began to tease him. The duckling hopped away, flopping in a crock of thick soup. Before he could upset anything else in the kitchen, the woodsman angrily tossed him out into the cold once more. One way or another, the duckling managed to keep himself alive as best he could through the rest of the winter.

And at last, as spring returned, the duckling felt a new strength in his wings.

One day he saw the same white birds on the lake. "I will join them," said the duckling bravely, "even if they should kill me for my ugliness." Swimming slowly into their midst, he bowed his head and begged them to kill him. But even as he pleaded, he saw his own reflection among the water lilies, and lo, he was as beautiful as they! The old swans bent their heads in admiration and welcome. The ugly duckling had become a proud young swan!

Rumpelstiltskin

Long ago, in a faraway kingdom, there lived a foolish miller who had a beautiful, clever daughter. The miller boasted about his daughter at every opportunity. One day, when the king was walking near the mill, the miller stopped him to tell him of his daughter's accomplishments. The king listened in silence until finally the miller happened to say, "And she can also spin straw into gold."

The king—who loved gold most particularly—immediately asked that the miller's daughter be brought to his castle.

The next day the king showed the girl a huge pile of straw and said, "You must spin this into gold by sunrise or you shall die."

As the king closed and locked the door, the girl began to weep. "Oh, what will happen to me?" she cried. "I do not know how to turn straw into gold."

Suddenly a strange, tiny man appeared before her. "I can help you," he said, "but what will you give me in return?"

"I will give you my necklace," the girl replied.

The tiny man set to work, and by sunrise all the straw was turned to gold. When the king saw this, he led the girl to a larger room with more straw in it and again ordered her to spin it into gold or die.

The tiny man appeared again and when the girl offered him her ring, he spun all the straw into gold by sunrise.

This time the king took the girl to an even larger room and promised that if she turned all the straw there into gold, she would never have to do it again, but would become his queen.

When the tiny man came now, the girl had nothing more to give him.

"Will you promise me your first child when you become queen?" he asked.

The girl agreed—and again all the straw became gold.

When the king saw the huge room filled with gold the next morning, he was quite delighted. He kept his promise to the girl and preparations were started at once for a grand wedding.

The new queen was very happy. She sent for her father and gave him some of the gold so that he could live comfortably.

Time went by and a lovely princess was born to the queen. The baby was very beautiful and the king and queen were happy and proud.

Some months later, as the queen was singing a lullaby to her baby, the tiny man who had helped her suddenly came into the room. The queen had quite forgotten him and her promise to him.

The little man said, "I have come to take your first child."

"Oh, no, no!" exclaimed the queen, and she burst into tears. She pleaded and pleaded with the tiny man to have mercy.

"I will give you three days to guess my name," the tiny man said at last. "If you do, you may keep your child. If you don't, I shall take her with me."

Then the tiny man was gone before the queen could dry her eyes.

The next day, when the tiny man returned, the queen started. "Albert?" "No." "Alan?" "No." "Ambrose?" "No, no." "Archibald?" The tiny man laughed. "Not that."

The queen kept guessing and guessing, calling all the names she knew beginning with A, then B, then C, and right through the alphabet to "Zweifach."

"Ha, ha!" laughed the little man. "You had better try harder tomorrow." And off he went.

The queen called all of the court messengers and told them to travel throughout the kingdom and bring back every unusual name they could find.

The next day she tried all of these on the tiny man.
"MacElwane?" "Thurston?" "Alcibades?" But all the tiny man did was laugh and say no.

When he left, the last of the queen's messengers returned. He apologized for coming back so late, but it seemed that he had been lost in the forest, where he saw an odd sight—a very small man dancing and singing,

"Today I bake,
    tomorrow I brew,
Today for one,
    tomorrow for two.
For how can she learn,
    my poor Royal Dame,
That Rumpelstiltskin
    is my name."

The queen was so happy, she gave the messenger a handful of gold.

The next day the tiny man came to the queen's room, and said, "I'm ready to listen to names all day long, but when I leave, I shall take your child."

The queen replied, "I've been trying too hard. Your name must be an easy one. Is it Sam?" "No, no!" shouted the little man gleefully. "Ben?" "No." "Adam?" "No, no, no."

At last she asked, "Could it be Rumpelstiltskin?"

Well, you should have seen that tiny man! He stamped his foot so angrily that he fell over backward.

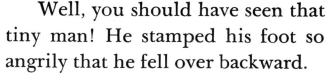

"A witch must have told you!" he shouted again and again. When he caught his breath, he rushed out of the room and the queen never saw him again.

The princess grew up to be as beautiful as the queen — and the king, the queen, and their daughter were truly happy.

The Princess and the Pea

Once upon a time there was a prince who wanted to marry a princess, but he wanted to be certain that she was a REAL princess.

He traveled all over the world in his search. There were many princesses, but he never could be sure that they were REAL princesses. There was always something that didn't seem quite right.

At last he came home, feeling very sad. He believed he never would find one to suit him.

One evening a terrible storm came up. The night was filled with lightning and the roar of thunder, and the rain streamed down. Suddenly there was a knocking at the gate, and the old king went out to open it.

It was a princess who stood outside. But what a state she was in! Water dripped from her hair and clothes; it ran in at the tops of her shoes and out at her heels. And yet she said that she was a real princess.

"Well, we shall soon find out whether she is or not," thought the queen.

She slipped into the bed chamber for royal guests, took off the bedding, and put a pea on the bedstead. Then twenty mattresses were placed on top of the pea, and twenty eider-down featherbeds upon the mattresses. This was to be the princess's bed for the night.

In the morning the queen asked her how she had slept.
"Oh, miserably!" answered the princess. "I scarcely closed my

eyes all night. Goodness only knows what was in my bed. I lay
upon something hard, so that I'm black and blue all over!''

"Here's your REAL princess!" the queen said to her son. "No one but a real princess is sensitive enough to feel a pea through twenty mattresses and twenty eider-down featherbeds."

So the prince joyfully asked her to be his wife, and they were married. And the pea was placed in the royal museum, where you may see it to this day, unless someone has stolen it.

Tom Thumb

There once lived a farmer and his wife who had all they wanted except a child of their own.

"If we only had a son," sighed the wife, "I would be content, even if he were no bigger than my thumb."

In time, their wish came true—they were blessed with a fine baby boy who was no bigger than the wife's thumb. "Tom Thumb" became his name.

One day the farmer went deep into the forest to chop wood. As he left the house, he spoke aloud. "If only I had someone to bring my horse and cart to me, I could haul the wood back tonight," he said.

Once the farmer was out of sight, Tom asked his mother to hitch the horse to the cart. Then, seating himself in the horse's ear, Tom told the horse exactly which way to go. Later that day, to the farmer's great surprise, his horse appeared, pulling the cart, but with no driver!

"Here I am, Father!" called Tom. "I have brought the cart, as you wished."

Now two wicked men had seen what Tom had done and at once began to think that they could gain much money by showing off the tiny boy at fairs. They offered the farmer a great deal of money for Tom. The father naturally refused, but Tom, hiding in his father's jacket, told him to agree, assuring his father that he would soon be home again. And so it was that Tom set out with the two men, riding on the hatbrim of one of them so that he could see the countryside as they traveled along.

When evening came, Tom called out, "Please, sirs, set me down. I am tired of riding up here." But as soon as the men had done this, Tom skipped off into the tall grass and disappeared down a mousehole.

The men were furious, but in the dark they could not find any trace of the boy, and so at last they lay down to rest for the night, grumbling at their bad luck. Once they were asleep, Tom crept out and, finding a snail shell under a fat toadstool, crawled in and was soon fast asleep.

The next morning he overheard the same two men discussing a robbery. "The squire has plenty of gold in his house," said one. "If only we could get in. . ."

"I can help you," called Tom.

The men were startled to hear his voice so close by and even more to discover tiny Tom in the snail shell. "How can YOU help us?" they asked, relieved to have found him once again.

"I'll slip in through the bars of the window and pass out to you whatever you want," replied Tom. And so it was agreed.

Off went the three to the squire's house. But no sooner was Tom inside than he called out in a loud voice. "What would you like me to hand to you first?"

"Hush!" cried the robbers. "You'll wake everyone!"

"I can't hear you!" shouted Tom, even louder than before. "Do you want me to pass out all the gold and silver to you?"

By this time the housemaid had been awakened from her sleep. Hearing the commotion, she soon guessed that thieves must be about, bent on stealing the squire's treasure.

Hopping out of bed, she dashed to the door and drove off the two men with a broom. Tom, being a clever boy, quietly slipped out of the house and crept away to the barn.

Early in the morning, the maid came to the barn to feed the cow. Before Tom Thumb could open his eyes, the maid had picked him up in a forkful of hay and the cow had swallowed him. He began to shout, "No more food, no more food!" and the maid thought the cow was bewitched.

The maid screamed for the squire, who came running. When he heard "No more food!" from the cow's mouth, he turned the cow out to pasture. Tom Thumb was able to slip out of the cow's mouth unnoticed. Once more he set out to find his way home. And because of his earlier ride atop the man's hat, he had no trouble in knowing which way to go.

But he soon grew tired and stopped to rest in the shade of a leaf. At that very moment a hungry wolf happened along and swallowed the boy in one gulp. Tom, however, did not lose courage. From the wolf's stomach he told the wolf that he knew of a place where a really fine meal could be found.

The greedy wolf was quite happy to follow Tom's directions, and in a short time he trotted up to the house of Tom Thumb's parents. Knowing that the farmer and his wife would be asleep, Tom told the wolf to creep in through a hidden opening.

Once inside the house, the wolf ate all the food in the pantry.

Having eaten his fill, the wolf turned to crawl out again. But now he had grown too fat to squeeze through the opening! Tom called out loudly for help. The wolf struggled to escape, but by this time the farmer had come out to the pantry to see what all the noise was about.

"Father! Save me!" cried Tom. "I'm here in the wolf's stomach."

In an instant the farmer felled the wolf and rescued his tiny son.

Then what a wonderful time they had together as Tom told of his adventures! His mother soon had him dressed in a fine new suit of clothes, and all three lived quite comfortably and happily for many, many years.

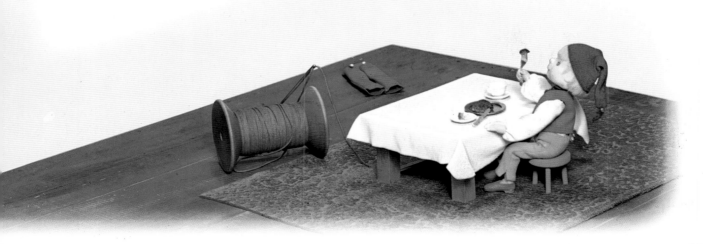